ALL ABOUT PIKACHU

SCHOLASTIC INC.

ISBN 978-1-338-27964-1

10 9 8 7 6 5 4 3 2 1   18 19 20 21 22

Printed in China 84
First printing 2018
Book design by Carolyn Bull

CONTENTS

Introducing . . . Pikachu! 4

How Pikachu Met Ash 8

Pikachu Fun Facts 12

Pikachu's Amazing Moves and Attacks 18

Pikachu and Pokémon Evolution 24

Pikachu's Wannabe Poachers 32

Pikachu Power 34

Pikachu vs. the Elite Four 40

Tournament Triumphs and Tribulations 44

Guess Who Likes to Bike? 48

Gotta Ketchup 'Em All 51

Who's That Pokémon? 52

Pikachu the Movie Star 54

Is That You, Pikachu? 57

Pikachu's Secret Crush 62

Pikachu's Heroes 64

Unexpected Team-Ups 66

Signature Strategies 70

Great Gym Battles 72

Pikachu's Got Moves—Z-Moves! 78

Isn't It Grand? 79

Conclusion 80

Pikachu: Mouse Pokémon
Type: Electric
Height: 1'04"
Weight: 13.2 lb.

INTRODUCING...
PIKACHU!

Who is Pikachu? Does this world-famous Pokémon even need an introduction? It is known all over the globe, but there is still so much to discover about this electrifying Pokémon.

Pikachu naturally stores up electricity in its body, and it needs to discharge that energy on a regular basis to maintain good health. To take advantage of this, some have suggested creating a Pikachu-fueled power plant.

Pikachu is bold, strong, resourceful, and, above all, loyal. It shows its strength on and off the battlefield. It's always there for a friend in need, and it isn't afraid to stand up to a foe—whether it's three members of Team Rocket or a pack of fellow Pokémon. Together with Ash, its Trainer and best friend, Pikachu is the kind of brave buddy who's game for any adventure and bold enough to fight for what's right!

Unlike most Pokémon, Pikachu refuses to travel in its Poké Ball. It prefers to ride perched on Ash's shoulder. This way, it's always ready for action.

Forget beauty sleep—the Mouse Pokémon needs a good night's rest for sheer battle strength. Pikachu's red cheeks are filled with electric power that recharges while it rests. So if you spot a sleeping Pikachu in the forest, be sure to keep quiet. You don't want to wake it up—it's important Pikachu gets its shut-eye!

Pikachu often zap first, ask questions later. Their first response to seeing new things and even people can be a Thunderbolt. So don't be shocked if you get shocked when you meet a wild Pikachu!

Want to know more about this amazing Pokémon? Read on! This book will give you a glimpse at all the special things that make Pikachu, well, Pikachu!

HOW PIKACHU MET ASH

Unlike most new Trainers, Ash didn't get the chance to pick his first partner Pokémon. He overslept and was late reaching Professor Oak's lab. When he finally arrived, all that was left was a feisty Pikachu who'd been returned by its Trainers.

Ash was certain he and Pikachu would have a blast together, but it turned out to be a different kind of blast than he was hoping for. When he gave Pikachu a big hug, Pikachu zapped him. Then Pikachu zapped Ash's mom and all his friends, too.

Ash was sure he could win Pikachu over. In the meantime, he wanted Pikachu to help him make his first Pokémon catch. When the little Electric-type refused, Ash was determined to do it on his own. He tried throwing a rock at a Spearow, but the Flying-type Pokémon thought Pikachu had hit it. Soon Spearow and a whole flock of Fearow were attacking Pikachu! Ash grabbed his injured first partner and ran for it.

Ash fled carrying Pikachu over a waterfall and through the woods. But when it started pouring rain, he couldn't run anymore. Ash turned to face the Fearow and Spearow. He begged them to leave Pikachu alone and fight him instead.

When he heard his Trainer defending him, Pikachu realized he had a true friend in Ash. His words give Pikachu the strength to unleash a terrific Thunderbolt.

In a flash, the whole flock retreated. Ash and Pikachu had worked together as an unstoppable team for the very first time!

Since then, Pikachu and Ash have tackled so many adventures, it's almost funny to remember their first impressions of each other. Ash thought he was just getting a first partner Pokémon. What he got was so much more: a best friend.

PIKACHU FUN FACTS

Want to get to know Pikachu a little better? Check out this terrific trivia!

1 Pikachu loves ketchup. It will pour it on anything, even a battle! It once used a bottle of ketchup to block a tough move, Cut, from Scyther.

2 Pikachu has rhythm! In a heated battle with the Anistar City Gym Leader, Olympia, Pikachu tapped its tail to keep the beat—and keep track of time for Ash.

3 No one gets rid of trouble and makes it double better than Pikachu! Using its incredible Thunderbolt, it's sent Team Rocket and their hot air balloon blasting off hundreds of times.

4 Ash and Pikachu are always ready to step up and help a Pokémon in need! When Team Rocket locked Professor Sycamore's pal Garchomp in a control collar, Pikachu cleverly used its Iron Tail to slash through the neck brace and free the giant Pokémon.

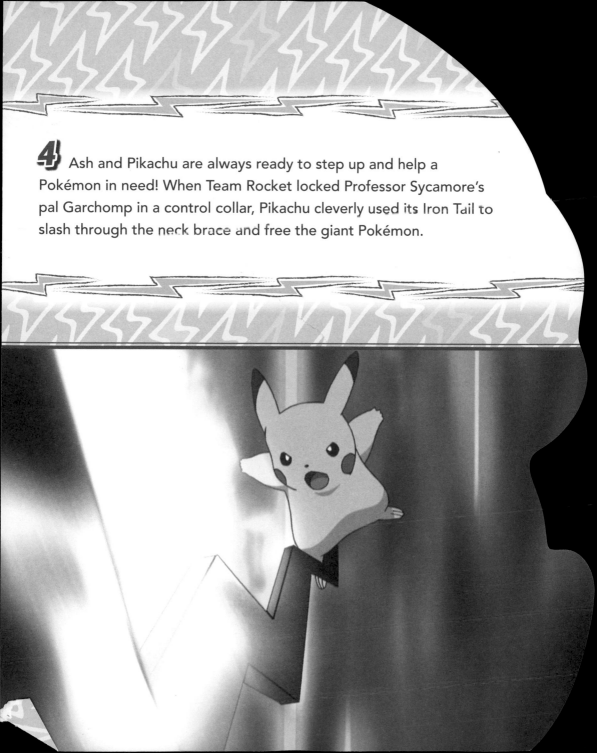

5 Pikachu can use its charm to help Ash out of even the most awkward situations. When Ash spotted Axew in the woods, he immediately tried to catch it, not realizing it had a Trainer already—Iris. But instead of getting mad, Iris got totally distracted by adorable Pikachu, and she decided to join them on their journey!

6 Pikachu is known for its Electric-type moves, but it also draws power from its self-esteem. When Pikachu decided not to evolve, it made a huge show of strength in battle. Even though Ash had the Thunderstone to help it evolve, Pikachu decided to be true to itself. Ash and Pikachu went on to win the battle against Raichu and its trash-talking Trainer, Sho.

PIKACHU'S AMAZING MOVES AND ATTACKS

So how does Pikachu manage to dominate in battle? Check out this list of its most powerful moves!

THUNDER SHOCK

is a zap of electricity sent over a foe.

THUNDERBOLT

is a jolt of electricity that surrounds Pikachu and then bursts on or around an opponent, hitting them with a sharp, bright blast.

If Pikachu has a need for speed,

AGILITY can help it.

QUICK ATTACK

has Pikachu racing toward a foe in a flash.

THUNDER

sends a Super Bolt straight down
from the sky to shock an opponent.

DOUBLE-EDGE

is a type of tackle that might be painful for a foe, but
also deals damage to Pikachu.

TACKLE

is simply lunging and
slamming into an opponent.

LEER is a fierce look that intimidates an opponent.

When Pikachu's tail glows with

IRON TAIL,

it becomes a solid weapon able to deliver a serious wallop.

VOLT TACKLE

covers Pikachu in an electric charge as it lunges at a foe.

With **ELECTRO BALL**, Pikachu shoots a shocking sphere at its enemy.

GIGAVOLT HAVOC

is an impressive Z-Move in which Pikachu and Ash move in sync, setting up a powerful punch that fires a giant burst of electric energy.

BREAKNECK BLITZ

is a bold Z-Move in which Pikachu, surrounded by a big burst of power, slams into an opponent, creating an explosion upon impact.

PIKACHU AND POKÉMON EVOLUTION

One of the things that makes Pikachu unique is that it has made the decision NOT to evolve.

When Pokémon evolve, the transformation is incredible. It can make a Pokémon bigger, stronger, and able to perform fierce new attacks and moves.

That kind of power can make a Pokémon more likely to win a battle, but it can't compare to the bond of friendship between a Trainer and its Pokémon pal. With that special connection comes support and understanding. It's the kind of bond a Trainer needs to let her Pokémon decide if and when it wants to evolve. Because once it does, there is no going back.

Here is the story of how Ash and Pikachu handled that important decision together.

PIKACHU AND A POWER SURGE

"I've come for a Pokémon battle. I want to earn a Thunder Badge!" Ash proclaimed as he entered the Vermillion Gym.

The Gym Leader, Lt. Surge, responded by giving Ash a noogie and calling him and Pikachu babies.

"Why are you making fun of my Pikachu?" Ash protested.

"I'll show you why!" Lt. Surge said. He indicated his battle partner, Raichu, the evolved form of Pikachu.

The Gym Leader told Ash that if he really were a serious Trainer, he would evolve his Pikachu to Raichu and then challenge him. Ash's friend Brock agreed with Lt. Surge—technically, Raichu *was* stronger than Pikachu.

But Pikachu was happy being Pikachu. It gathered its courage, and soon it was ready to stand up to this big bully on the battlefield! Pikachu's cheeks buzzed with electricity. It couldn't wait to begin the round with Raichu and Lt. Surge.

"*Pika, pika!*" Pikachu shouted, excited for the chance to prove its power.

Pikachu struck first, sending a terrific Thunder Shock across the battlefield. But Raichu didn't even flinch. It showed off its much, much stronger Thunder Shock. It looked like Ash and Pikachu were in way over their heads.

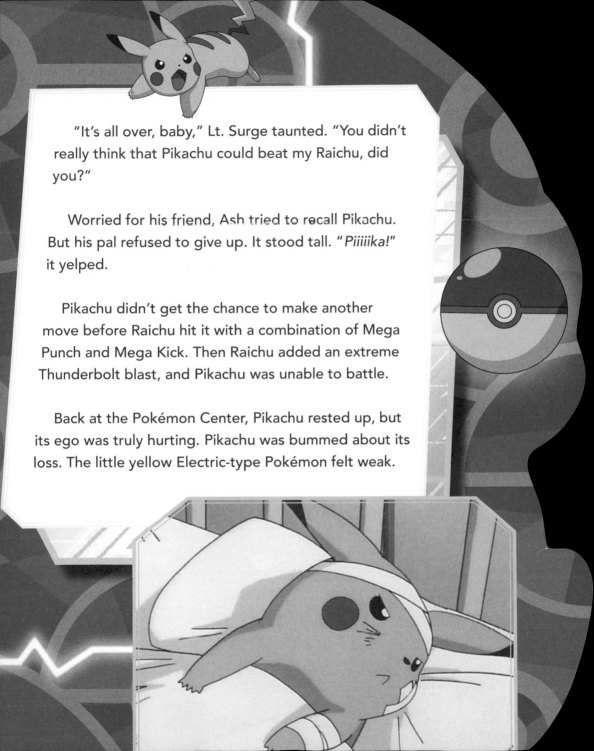

"It's all over, baby," Lt. Surge taunted. "You didn't really think that Pikachu could beat my Raichu, did you?"

Worried for his friend, Ash tried to recall Pikachu. But his pal refused to give up. It stood tall. "*Piiiiika!*" it yelped.

Pikachu didn't get the chance to make another move before Raichu hit it with a combination of Mega Punch and Mega Kick. Then Raichu added an extreme Thunderbolt blast, and Pikachu was unable to battle.

Back at the Pokémon Center, Pikachu rested up, but its ego was truly hurting. Pikachu was bummed about its loss. The little yellow Electric-type Pokémon felt weak.

The Pokémon Center's caretaker, Nurse Joy, overheard Ash trying to cheer Pikachu up. She offered Ash a precious Thunderstone—exactly what Pikachu needed to evolve.

But as Nurse Joy handed Ash the Thunderstone, she warned him, "You've got to think hard before using this."

Ash considered this important decision. Perhaps as Raichu, Pikachu would be able to win a rematch with Lt. Surge. The offer was tempting, and with it came added power on the battlefield.

On the other hand, Ash worried that if he made Pikachu evolve, well, then he'd be a bully just like Lt. Surge. Ash knew the decision belonged to Pikachu.

"Do you want to be Raichu?" Ash asked his best pal.

Pikachu paused to think for a moment. Then it stood up in its bed and knocked the stone out of Ash's hand.

Pikachu was happy just the way it was. If it was going to beat Raichu, it was going to do it as Pikachu!

Ash was so proud of his buddy. The rematch battle might be hard, but nothing was impossible as long as they were together!

"Pikachu and I will find a way to win!" Ash vowed.

"*Pika, pika!*" Pikachu cheered.

Ash began planning his battle strategy for the rematch with Lt. Surge. Brock pointed out that Lt. Surge immediately evolved Raichu, so it never really spent time training as Pikachu. That advantage could be their path to victory!

Pikachu and Ash marched back to the Vermillion Gym to challenge Lt. Surge. The Gym Leader was very surprised to see Pikachu again. But when he saw Ash hadn't made Pikachu evolve, he was confident their second battle would end the same way as their first did.

At first, it looked like Lt. Surge was right. Raichu dominated the beginning of the battle, slapping Pikachu with its tail and crushing it with Body Slam. Pikachu didn't seem to have a chance, but Ash reminded it to stick to their strategy.

When Raichu tried Body Slam again, Ash told Pikachu to use Agility to dodge the attack. It worked! Raichu evolved too fast to learn the speed attacks from the Pikachu stage. So Pikachu decided to make its attacks fast and furious!

Raichu tried to knock Pikachu out with its incredibly powerful Thunderbolt. The attack was so strong, it broke all the windows in the Gym, but it didn't stop Pikachu. Ash's Pokémon quickly used its tail as a ground and dodged the move.

Raichu tried to use Thunderbolt again, but it was tapped out. So Ash asked Pikachu to finish the round with Quick Attack. Thanks to Pikachu's speed and courage, it won the rematch!

Impressed with their teamwork and strategy, Lt. Surge awarded Pikachu a Thunder Badge.

"You should be proud," Lt. Surge told Ash. "You and your Pikachu really fought well together."

From that day on, Pikachu never saw a reason to evolve or be anybody but itself. On their journey, Ash and Pikachu have encountered many challenges, but they know they can climb any mountain, solve any puzzle, and win any match as long as they believe in themselves.

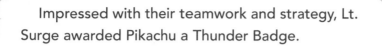

PIKACHU'S WANNABE POACHERS

Pokémon thieves Team Rocket—Jessie, James, and Meowth—are obsessed with poaching Pokémon. Sure, they'll steal any Pokémon, but their number-one pick is the powerful Pikachu.

Team Rocket has followed Ash through every region in the hopes of nabbing his pal Pikachu. The trio has tried everything from simple straw traps to highly sophisticated mechas, but Pikachu always slips through their greedy paws and foils their plans. One of Pikachu's favorite pastimes is sending Team Rocket blasting off again!

PIKACHU POWER

Pikachu is a pretty powerful Pokémon. It's always charged up and ready to battle! But in a few important fights, Pikachu managed to become even stronger. This loyal little Electric-type Pokémon always uses its might to do what's right. Read on to discover the stories of some of Pikachu's best battles.

TEAM MAGMA & TEAM AQUA ARE NO MATCH FOR TEAM PIKACHU

While trying to stop evil Team Magma and Team Aqua from destroying the delicate balance between the Sea Basin Pokémon, Kyogre, and the Continent Pokémon, Groudon, Pikachu caught the treasured Blue Orb. The sphere fused with its body, and its face glowed with a red pattern.

Pikachu had an incredible power, but it couldn't control that power. Groudon asked for Pikachu's help and Pikachu sent Team Rocket blasting off, channeled a lightning storm, teamed up with Groudon to defeat Kyogre, destroyed Team Aqua and Team Magma's plans, and restored order. That's a whole lot of power in a little Pikachu!

TURNED UP BY THUNDURUS

When Team Rocket trapped Meloetta and summoned Tornadus, Thundurus, and Landorus, Pikachu stepped up in a battle of epic proportions. Its mission: to save its friends and Unova from falling into the hands of Team Rocket's leader, Giovanni.

When a fierce bolt from Thundurus headed straight for his friend Iris, Pikachu jumped in to protect her. Amazingly, the electricity from Thundurus's attack actually powered up Pikachu. Using its increased strength, it fired a huge Electro Ball that stopped Team Rocket and set Meloetta free.

WATTS UP?!

Spunky Mauville Gym Leader Wattson has a roller coaster ride as the entrance to his Gym. When Ash and his pals arrived, Wattson pranked them by turning up the power to give the ride extra oomph.

During the ride, a fierce robot Raikou jumped out at the crew. It was so realistic, Ash asked Pikachu to step in. When Pikachu landed a tough Iron Tail right between its eyes, Pikachu wound up getting supercharged.

At first, Pikachu seemed just fine, so it was shocking that it won the match against Wattson and all his incredible Electric-type Pokémon pals with just a single strike. Ash was awarded the Dynamo Badge, but something didn't seem right. Ash soon discovered that Pikachu had a fever and rushed it to the Pokémon Center. There Nurse Joy told Ash that Pikachu was overcharged.

That's when Ash realized the robot Raikou must have given Pikachu surplus juice—and an advantage in his Gym battle. Like a good sport, Ash apologized to Wattson and told him the truth about his easy win. Impressed with his honesty, Wattson let Ash keep his Gym Badge.

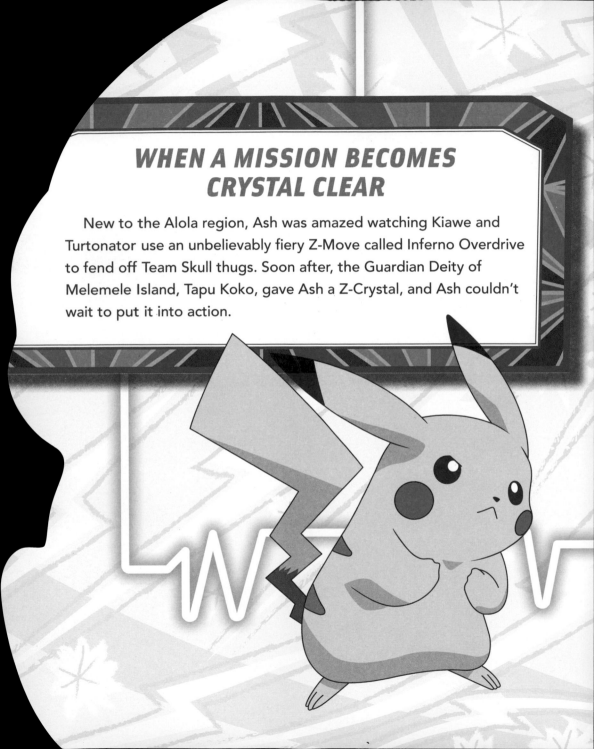

WHEN A MISSION BECOMES CRYSTAL CLEAR

New to the Alola region, Ash was amazed watching Kiawe and Turtonator use an unbelievably fiery Z-Move called Inferno Overdrive to fend off Team Skull thugs. Soon after, the Guardian Deity of Melemele Island, Tapu Koko, gave Ash a Z-Crystal, and Ash couldn't wait to put it into action.

During their battle, Ash and Pikachu channeled the power of Electrium Z to create their first Z-Move, a big blast of electric energy—Gigavolt Havoc.

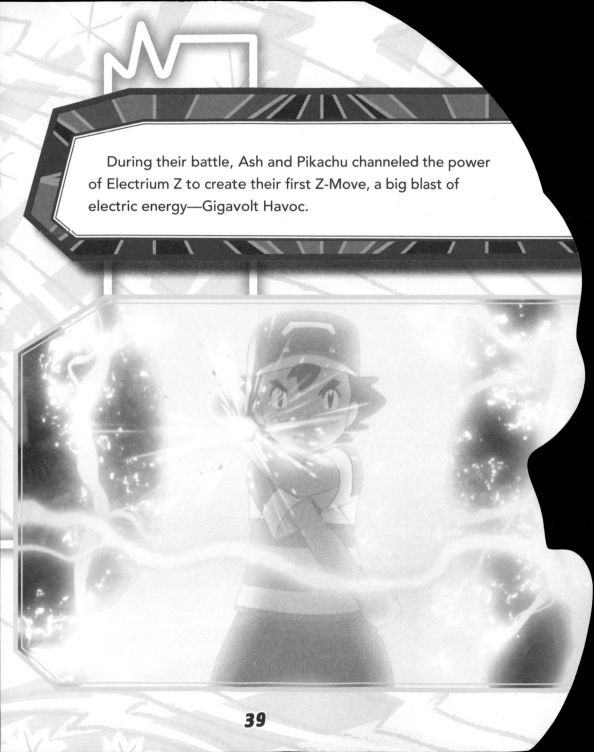

PIKACHU vs. THE ELITE FOUR

One of Pikachu's greatest battle accomplishments came when the little Electric-type got to strut its stuff against the world-famous Elite Four! They are considered the four toughest, most skilled Trainers in their regions.

REGION: *HOENN*
ELITE FOUR MEMBER: *DRAKE*

Aboard Drake's ship, Pikachu battled Shelgon. Although it seemed Pikachu was dominating the match, it turned out to be a trick. Once Pikachu got close to Shelgon, Pikachu was served a surprise and got knocked out.

REGION: *KANTO*
ELITE FOUR MEMBER: *AGATHA*

When Ash got the opportunity to battle Viridian Gym Leader and Elite Four member Agatha, he confidently called on his best buddy, Pikachu. But the Electric-type Pokémon had a big disadvantage battling a Ghost-type like Gengar. Agatha and Gengar won the match, but Agatha was impressed by Ash and Pikachu's battle spirit. Win or lose, they got an A for effort!

REGION: *SINNOH*
ELITE FOUR MEMBER: *FLINT*

Ash tried to challenge the Sunyshore Gym Leader Volkner to a battle, but Elite Four Member Flint wound up accepting the challenge. Pikachu battled boldly against Flint's Infernape. While it lost the match, Pikachu won over Volkner, and he agreed to battle Ash for the Beacon Badge. At their match, Pikachu won a round against Volkner's Electivire.

REGION: *UNOVA*
ELITE FOUR MEMBER: *ALDER*

When Alder accepted Ash and Pikachu's battle challenge, it was a dream come true for Ash and Pikachu. However, Alder was the one dreaming—he fell asleep right in the middle of the battle! Alder's Bouffalant was not happy. But both the nap and the battle were interrupted by an injured Gigalith. The Elite Four hero had to call off the battle and snap into action to save the hurt giant— with a little help from Ash and Pikachu.

REGION: *KALOS*
ELITE FOUR MEMBER: *DIANTHA*

They say the way to someone's heart is through their stomach . . . and that's how Ash got movie star and Kalos Champion Diantha to agree to battle him: by sharing his piece of chocolate cake with her! Ash called on his best buddy, Pikachu, for the match. Unfortunately, the battle was cut short by a Team Rocket attack.

TOURNAMENT TRIUMPHS AND TRIBULATIONS

If there's one thing Pikachu has in spades, it's grit. The little yellow Pokémon really packs a punch when he's battling in tournaments. Check out what happened at some of his toughest competitions!

INDIGO CONFERENCE

Ash called on Pikachu to battle Jeanette and her Bellsprout, but he underestimated the Flower Pokémon's power. In a surprise upset, Pikachu's Thunderbolts just couldn't break through and Bellsprout won the round.

JOHTO SILVER CONFERENCE

After defeating his rival Gary, Ash was set to face
Harrison in the Final 8. So, of course, he called on his best
buddy, Pikachu. The Electric-type gave the battle its all
and won the match against Harrison's Kecleon. But when
Sneasel stepped in, weary Pikachu was unable to continue.

EVER GRANDE TOURNAMENT

In the one-on-one
preliminary match, Pikachu
sealed a win, advancing Ash
to the next round.

LILY OF THE VALLEY CONFERENCE

In the Quarter Finals of the Sinnoh League, Ash chose Pikachu first to fight his rival Paul. But when a burst of Aggron's Flash Cannon stopped Pikachu's Volt Tackle in its tracks, Ash switched out his best buddy for Infernape.

KALOS LEAGUE TOURNAMENT

In the Semifinal of the Kalos League, Ash was pitted against Sawyer. For his third Pokémon pick, Ash called on Pikachu. In the round with Clawitzer, Pikachu escaped its grasp with a shocking combination of Electro Ball and Thunderbolt. Next, Sawyer called on Aegislash, the Royal Sword Pokémon. While Aegislash used King's Shield to weaken Pikachu, Ash's clever strategy proved Pikachu was unstoppable. First he had Pikachu use Iron Tail to toss the chopped trees on the battlefield up in the air. Then he used the logs to jam Aegislash's shield. Finally, with a single, strong Thunderbolt, Pikachu won the round.

GUESS WHO LIKES TO BIKE?

Food lovers might argue that everything is better fried, but some of Ash's friends would disagree when it comes to their rides. Misty, May, and Dawn all had their two-wheelers zapped to a crisp by Pikachu's Thunderbolt. So bike owners, beware of parking near Pikachu!

MISTY   *"HEY, THAT'S MY BIKE!"*

While fishing for Water-type Pokémon one day, Misty accidentally hooked two new friends—Ash and Pikachu. The pair rode off on her bike as they fled a flock of Spearow and Fearow. Then Pikachu fired a Thunder Shock so strong, it burned Misty's bike. But Ash and Pikachu soon restored the torched two-wheeler. Misty got a newly refinished bike, plus a couple of cool travel partners to ride with!

MAY *"MY BIKE'S BARBECUED!"*

When Team Rocket's plan backfired—literally—May's bike got caught in the cross fire. Pikachu was overcharged and feeling under the weather. A Team Rocket mecha planned to drain it of its power, but the machine couldn't handle all of powered-up Pikachu's electricity. Amazingly enough, the mecha managed to heal Pikachu and restore it to normal. The second it was feeling up to snuff, Pikachu blasted off Team Rocket and the mecha with a Thunderbolt so strong, it zapped May's bike, too.

DAWN *"MY BIKE! IT'S EXTRA CRISPY!"*

After witnessing the power of Pikachu's Thunderbolt on her bike, Dawn had one thing on her mind. She didn't care about her ride, she just wanted to catch the rad Pokémon that is Pikachu. Of course, Pikachu already had a Trainer. And as the old saying goes, if you can't catch 'em, join 'em.

GOTTA KETCHUP 'EM ALL

Pikachu loves ketchup. And not just on food—it also finds it quite useful in battle!

Pikachu and its most beloved condiment had Scyther seeing red during their match. Because of its fiery color, the very sight of the delicious sauce makes Scyther mad. During their heated battle in Dark City, Pikachu even used the ketchup bottle as a shield, blocking Scyther's Cut!

WHO'S THAT POKÉMON?

Pikachu is a master at mimicking other Pokémon. At the Sinnoh Region's annual Pokémon dress-up contest, it got the chance to show off its skills. Instead of wearing a costume, Pikachu transformed itself with incredible impressions Ash calls "shape copying." In seconds, Pikachu became Seviper, Wobbuffet, Buneary, Mudkip, Lotad, and Loudred. Pikachu got loads of applause, and it was happy to soak it all in!

PIKACHU THE MOVIE STAR

PLUS THE COSPLAY PIKACHU CO-STARS

While traveling through Kalos, Ash, Serena, Bonnie, Clemont, and Pikachu stumbled upon an amazing place—Pikachu Manor, home to dozens of Pikachu and their biggest fan, Frank. Since he was a boy, Frank dreamed of sharing the joy of Pikachu with a movie audience. The minute he spotted Ash's pal Pikachu, Frank knew he'd found a star!

Frank enlisted Pikachu to act alongside some top Pikachu talent: Pikachu Belle; Pikachu, PhD; Pikachu Libre; Pikachu Rock Star; and Pikachu Pop Star.

In the film, Pikachu played a superhero with wings that would risk everything to save a special place called Pikachuland. Super Pikachu bravely battled back a pack of Pikachu bent on taking over the whole town. The ending might not shock you, but it sure shocked the villains!

In the movie, Ash's pal Pikachu was the first to stand up and fight, but it was soon joined by the citizens of Pikachuland. Together, the pack of brave Pikachu sent the bullies blasting off with a massive electric explosion.

Would Pikachu's first film be a box office smash or a cult classic? One thing is for sure: Super Pikachu is a superstar!

IS THAT YOU, PIKACHU?

There are Pokémon out there who may look like Pikachu, act like Pikachu, and sometimes even say *"Pika"* like Pikachu . . . *but they are not Pikachu!* Yes, it's true: The world is full of Pikachu wannabes! After all, who wouldn't want to be the world's favorite yellow friend?

Have no fear; true Pikachu fans will see through the fakers. Here are a few infamous Pikachu impersonators.

MIMIKYU

MIMIKYU: Disguise Pokémon
Type: Ghost-Fairy
Height: 0'08"
Weight: 1.5 lb.

The Disguise Pokémon wears a cloth costume that looks like Pikachu for two reasons. One, it wants to hide what it looks like. Two, it hopes looking like Pikachu will help it make friends, since everyone loves the Mouse Pokémon.

Deep down, lonely Mimikyu is afraid to show its true self. Not much is really known about this mysterious Pokémon. It is rumored that someone once saw it without its disguise, and that was the end of him.

When Team Rocket's Meowth first met this mysterious Pokémon, he sneaked a peek under its rag—and immediately got sucked into a nightmare! But Meowth would probably say that Mimikyu's true feelings about Pikachu are even scarier than his dream. You see, Mimikyu doesn't actually like Pikachu. Perhaps Mimikyu's costume should be green with envy!

Underneath Mimikyu's soft, fabric exterior is a terrifically tough Pokémon. In fact, when Ash asked Pikachu to help him catch Mimikyu, Mimikyu easily overpowered the Pokémon it was mimicking. It seems Pikachu has met its match in Mimikyu.

Once, Mimikyu's outfit got ripped while Team Rocket was blasting off. Jessie tried to take it shopping for new clothes, but Mimikyu refused every option. There's only one frock for this Pokémon—faux Pikachu. So Jessie stitched up the hole, and Mimikyu resumed its disguise.

IMPOSTER #2:
ASH?!

When Ash and Pikachu met a Pokémon Magician, they volunteered to assist her with a new spell that would give a Trainer the ability to read Pokémon minds. Amazingly enough, the final piece of the spell was a jolt of Pikachu's powerful Thunderbolt.

To Ash and Pikachu, casting this spell seemed noble—it could help improve the partnership between people and Pokémon. But when Pikachu polished off all the ingredients, it wound up getting shocked. When the cloud of smoke cleared, Ash had turned into Pikachu!

Fortunately, once the spell wore off, Ash returned to his human form. But while he was Pikachu, he relished his time playing with his Pokémon pals.

IMPOSTER #3:
HAWLUCHA

While making a movie about Pikachuland, the star Pikachu had some pretty difficult stunts. Namely, Pikachu had to fly. Rather than risk his best buddy's neck, Ash had his Flying-type friend Hawlucha dress up like Super Pikachu. Then he stepped up—er, that is, *sailed* up into the sky. When you have talented Pokémon pals, you don't need CGI. They can make their own movie magic!

♥ PIKACHU'S SECRET CRUSH

By now, you know a lot about Pikachu. You know Pikachu adores its best buddy, Ash. You know its favorite condiment is ketchup. But it keeps its crush a bit more of a secret.

But when it comes to keeping feelings on the down-low, Pikachu is no match for Misty. She figured out who Pikachu had feelings for, and even used that knowledge to her advantage!

When Ash and Misty both wanted to catch Totodile, there was only one way to settle it—with a Pokémon battle. Naturally, Ash picked Pikachu, so Misty confidently called on Togepi. But Pikachu refused to battle its beloved Spike Ball Pokémon. For her first move, Misty had Togepi give Pikachu a big hug. Then she ordered Togepi to turn on Charm.

Surrounded by swirling hearts, Pikachu broke into a sweat and ran off, forfeiting the battle. Ah, love makes us all do silly things!

PIKACHU'S HEROES

Even a heroic Pokémon like Pikachu needs someone to look up to! Read about some of the people and Pokémon that have inspired Pikachu.

PUKA, THE SURFER DUDE PIKACHU

In Kanto, there is a blue-eyed rider of waves known as Puka, the surfing Pikachu. According to Victor, its Trainer, Puka can sense big waves and how they're going to break.

Puka can also sense trouble. When Ash wiped out on his surfboard, Puka was the one who spotted him. It immediately sprang into action, and surfed up with Victor to save Ash.

Victor and Puka are an unsinkable team. Together, they've even surfed the legendary Humungadunga! Because of Puka's bravery, skill, and heart, Pikachu is a big fan of its ocean-loving pal.

SPARKY

Ash's friend Richie is pals with a Pikachu named Sparky. Sparky has a lot of flair and a tuft of blond hair—it's easy to spot because of its bangs. Like Ash's Pikachu, it likes to travel on its Trainer's shoulder.

Pikachu and Sparky really see eye to eye and are buds through and through. They became instant friends when they met at the Kanto Pokémon League. Together, the two Pikachu pals battled back Team Rocket.

A PACK OF PIKACHU

In the forest of Kanto, there's a special place rarely seen by people. Next to a waterfall and some apple trees lives a pack of Pikachu. And Pikachu made so many new Pikachu friends there. But there's only one Ash, and so Pikachu decided to stay with its Trainer and continue their journey.

UNEXPECTED TEAM-UPS

Pikachu is always by Ash's side. As a team, they always offer to help others. Sometimes that means battling together, and sometimes that can mean working with another Trainer or Pokémon for a common goal. Here are a couple of times Pikachu has partnered up to do some good!

SWEET AS SUGAR: *ABIGAIL & PIKACHU*

Elderly baker Abigail was distraught when her Pikachu, nicknamed Sugar, went missing. So her granddaughter begged Pikachu to play the part of her grandmother's missing best friend. Pikachu agreed to the act to help Abigail enter a baking contest. The plan worked like a charm . . . until Abigail challenged Ash to a battle with his own Pikachu! Fortunately, it turned out to be a trick. Abigail figured out Pikachu wasn't Sugar. And even luckier, Sugar returned as Raichu and arrived just in time to save Pikachu from Team Rocket.

PRINCE OF A GUY:
MISTY & PIKACHU

Misty entered the Princess Festival in the hopes of winning the grand prize: a one-of-a-kind collection of Pokémon Princess dolls. There was just one problem: She needed four Pokémon to qualify. Her pal Psyduck stepped in, and Misty borrowed Ash's buddies Pikachu and Bulbasaur plus Brock's pal Vulpix.

Ash warned Misty that Pokémon won't just listen to any Trainer—they need the bond of trust and true friendship. Misty proved herself worthy, and with the help of Pikachu and her travel companions, she won the match and the prize she'd dreamed of!

ATTACHED AT THE HIP: *MEOWTH & PIKACHU*

While traveling through Mandarin Island, a Team Rocket trap landed Ash and his pals in a ditch. When Pikachu tried to fight back, Meowth sneaked up with a special chain that bound the two Pokémon together!

Team Rocket escaped with Pikachu, but they didn't get very far before a wild Pidgeot snagged Pikachu and Meowth. Up high in the sky, far from its pals, Meowth panicked. Fortunately, Pikachu was there to use its super Thunderbolt to release them.

Pikachu and Meowth fell back down to the forest, but they were still stuck together. When an angry Rhydon started to chase them, the two Pokémon had to work as a team. Meowth used a Tickle Attack to get Rhydon's mouth open, and then Pikachu fired Thunderbolt past its chompers. The clever combination not only knocked out Rhydon, it also united Meowth and Pikachu . . . for now.

Later that night, the two Pokémon spotted a single apple atop a tree. Meowth wanted to eat it all, but Pikachu snagged it first. To Meowth's surprise, Pikachu chopped the apple in half and shared it. Meowth was so touched by the sweet, simple gesture, it changed its whole opinion of Pikachu.

Shortly thereafter, the two Pokémon were rescued by their friends. Although Meowth and Pikachu went their separate ways, for just one day, foes became friends.

SIGNATURE STRATEGIES

Ash and Pikachu are known for their clever battle strategies. Sometimes Pikachu even uses an attack or move on itself! Instead of firing at a foe, the Mouse Pokémon occasionally blasts itself or dives directly into its opponent's shot. Sure, this strategy doesn't seem to make sense, but it's just so crazy it works—and how! Pikachu has let itself be attacked and won a number of times:

In the final round of Ash's rematch at the Santalune Gym, Pikachu broke Vivillon's Sleep Powder slumber with a wake-up call from its own Electro Ball. Then, in a flash of Thunderbolt, Pikachu won the match, earning Ash the Bug Badge.

In a double battle, Ash wisely asked Pikachu to use Thunder on itself and Swellow. The electric field helped them fight right through Lunatone and Solrock's tough shield of Light Screen. It became the turning point of the electrifying battle, and Ash earned the Mind Badge thanks to the smart strategy.

When challenging the Castelia Gym Leader, Burgh, Ash and Pikachu found themselves in a sticky situation. Leavanny had Pikachu trapped in a tight wrap of its gooey String Shot. Pikachu's hands were truly tied. So when Leavanny went to fire Leaf Storm to finish the match, Ash had Pikachu jump right into the sharp, swirling greens. Surprisingly enough, Leaf Storm shredded right through the thread. Pikachu then went on to win the match with a big Electro Ball burst.

GREAT GYM BATTLES

Pikachu might be small, but it's had some truly big wins! The opponent that underestimates this Electric-type will find themselves shocked—most likely with a jolt of one of Pikachu's amazing electric attacks!

These fierce foes tangled with Pikachu and learned exactly how strong the little Pokémon truly is.

ROCK-SOLID ROUND AT PEWTER GYM
PIKACHU vs. GEODUDE + ONIX

Pikachu won the round with Geodude, but it seemed overwhelmed by gigantic Onix. Gym Leader Brock was about to back off the battle because he didn't want to hurt Pikachu. But suddenly, the sprinklers went off, and the water weakened Onix, giving Pikachu an advantage. So Pikachu seized the opportunity to claim a victory! Ash earned the Boulder Badge and another travel buddy: Gym Leader Brock decided to join Ash and Pikachu on their journey.

PIKACHU ON ICE AT THE BATTLE PYRAMID
PIKACHU vs. REGICE

They say the third time's the charm, but when the battle is on ice, it's more fun to say thrice. When Ash battled Frontier Brain Brandon and his Legendary Pokémon pal Regice, two losses didn't stop him. In their third match, Regice turned the Mouse Pokémon into an ice cube. Ash shouted to Pikachu to use Thunderbolt to melt itself out. And wouldn't you know it, the move heated up the battle and Pikachu roared back with a fierce Volt Tackle.

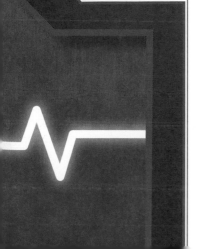

WHEN SOMETHING SOUR TURNS SWEET
PIKACHU + CHARIZARD vs. MAROWAK + ALAKAZAM

In this double battle with Gym Leader Luana and her Pokémon pals Marowak and Alakazam, Ash paired up Pikachu and Charizard. At first, they seemed more like enemies. But Pikachu stepped up to protect Charizard when it looked nearly crushed, and in that moment, the tide of the battle and their friendship turned. Together as a team, Charizard and Pikachu earned the Jade Star Badge.

WHERE THERE'S SMOG, THERE'S FIRE
PIKACHU vs. SLUGMA

After Treecko and Corphish battled Slugma, Ash sent in Pikachu at his battle against the brand-new Lavaridge Gym Leader Flannery. When Slugma sent a haze of Smog over the field, Pikachu used Thunderbolt to charge Slugma's Smog cloud. Then Pikachu sealed a win with a cutting clap of Thunder.

A MODEL BATTLE
PIKACHU vs. EMOLGA + TYNAMO

Battling Nimbasa Gym Leader Elesa, an Electric-type expert and supermodel, is always a challenge. But Ash and his best buddy, Pikachu, were ready to turn the battlefield into their runway! After Emolga won rounds against Snivy and Palpitoad, Pikachu stepped in. At first, it seemed like an even match between the two as they both used equally impressive Electro Balls. But when Pikachu added a speedy Quick Attack, it won the round. Next, it faced Tynamo, who buried Pikachu in the ground to lash and bash. Pikachu wriggled free and cleverly sent out Thunderbolt to recharge itself. Now fully energized, Pikachu doubled up on its incredible Iron Tail to win the round.

CLIMB EVERY MOUNTAIN
PIKACHU vs. TYRUNT

Climbing the mountain to get to the Cyllage City Gym seemed like a struggle until Gym Leader Grant took out his even tougher Tyrunt. It won rounds against Ash's Pokémon friends Froakie and Fletchling. For his last Pokémon, Ash picked his best pal, Pikachu. When Tyrunt fired mighty Draco Meteor, Pikachu used a new move called the "Draco Meteor Climb" to step up and dodge the attack. Surprised, Tyrunt tried another attack—Rock Tomb. Pikachu treated the attacks like baseballs and turned Iron Tail into a bat. Then it unleashed an amazing Thunderbolt burst to win the match!

PIKACHU'S GOT MOVES— Z-MOVES!

In the Alola region, Ash and Pikachu have proven themselves to be an impressive team. Among their new friends is the Guardian Deity of Melemele Island, Tapu Koko. After giving Ash a Z-Ring and an Electrium Z Z-Crystal, Tapu Koko challenged Ash to a battle. During their face-off, Tapu Koko encouraged Ash and Pikachu to put their Z-Ring to use and try to do a Z-Move.

For the first time, Ash and Pikachu danced in sync to power up their first, explosive Gigavolt Havoc. *Boom*! A black cloud taller than the trees covered the area. Even Pikachu couldn't believe its power! It truly took its bond with its Trainer to a whole new level.

ISN'T IT GRAND?

When it was time for Ash to have his first Grand Trial against the kahuna of Melemele Island, Ash called on his best pal, Pikachu. Kahuna Hala chose the hard-hitting Fighting-type Hariyama, and Pikachu's usual attacks had no effect against it.

But although Pikachu isn't as big or powerful as Hariyama, it's got speed on its side. With Quick Attack, Pikachu was able to avoid Hariyama's Z-Move, All-Out Pummeling. So Ash decided it was time for Pikachu to respond with the Z-Move Breakneck Blitz. This stunning show of strength earned Ash another Z-Crystal.

Although Ash was hoping for Fightinium Z, Tapu Koko presented Ash and Pikachu with Electrium Z. Pikachu was excited—this meant it would get to use Gigavolt Havoc again. So while the Grand Trial was over, it was a whole new beginning for Ash, Pikachu, and their Z-Moves!

CONCLUSION

This may be the end of the book, but you certainly don't have to end your adventures with Pikachu. There's no good-bye when it comes to that awesome yellow guy. Because as every Pokémon fan knows, there's always more fun in store with Pikachu!

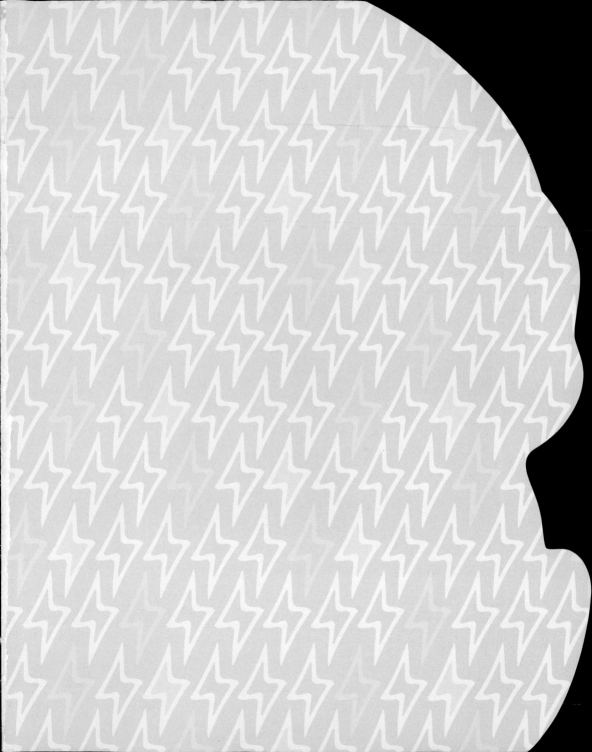